HACK ATTACK

<Written by>: Thomas Kingsley Troupe
<Illustrated by>: Scott Burroughs

www.12StoryLibrary.com

12-Story Library is an imprint of Peterson Publishing Company and Press Room Editions.

Produced for 12-Story Library by Red Line Editorial

Illustrations by Scott Burroughs
Technology adviser: Greg Case

ISBN
978-1-63235-229-3 (hardcover)
978-1-63235-254-5 (paperback)
978-1-62143-279-1 (hosted ebook)

Library of Congress Control Number: 2015934333

Printed in the United States of America
Mankato, MN
October, 2015

TABLE OF CONTENTS

chapter 1	That's Game!	5
chapter 2	Always Something	13
chapter 3	Bad Report	21
chapter 4	Not the Only One	30
chapter 5	Glitched!	38
chapter 6	Algorithms	47
chapter 7	Surprise!	55
chapter 8	Confession	64

Think About It	76
Write About It	77
About the Author	78
About the Illustrator	79
More Fun with The Coding Club	80

1

THAT'S GAME!

"Let's go, Badgers!" Coach Olson shouted from the bench. "Hold on to it!"

Grady Hopkins wasn't a great basketball player—at least he didn't think so. Even so, he was good enough to get on a youth traveling basketball team organized by the parks and recreation board. With a laid-back practice schedule and games every Saturday morning, it didn't interfere with the coding club Grady was part of after school. And although he didn't know BASIC, a programming language other kids in the coding club used, at least he knew the basics of basketball.

Just for fun, the park board put together a local championship of the traveling teams, pitting the different counties' teams against each other. Through a series of close games and a forfeiture or two, Grady's team, the Brock County Badgers, battled against the Wilbur County Wildcats for the championship.

Now that it was nearly the end of the fourth quarter, there was no getting around it; Grady was exhausted. The remaining two guys sitting on the bench were wiped, too. They'd played mediocre basketball up to the championship round. But now that there was a chance they could win it all, Grady realized no one on his team was in any condition to play as hard as the Wildcats. The Wildcats had won the last three years in a row, under the guidance of their leader, the stern-looking Coach Dremble.

Coach Olson called a time-out and the Badgers trotted over. Grady was ready to collapse.

"Okay, you guys are looking a little tired out there," Coach Olson said, passing the parks and recreation water bottles around. "We've got just a few minutes left on the clock. You keep these guys in line and we're walking away from this thing as champions."

"I'm so tired," a forward named Brett Robbins groaned.

"Me too," Grady agreed. "I'm not sure I even want to win."

Coach Olson shook his head and lightly bonked both Brett and Grady on the head with his clipboard. "Snap out of it, guys! This is the big game! The championship! We win this and Coach Dremble doesn't get his four-peat. We have to shut 'em down!"

Grady took a deep breath and let it out. For good measure, he blasted his face with some lukewarm water from a bottle. Then he looked up at the scoreboard. It was 54–48. The Badgers had a six-point lead.

A few more minutes, Hopkins, he told himself, feeling invigorated by Coach's pep talk. *We got this.*

The referee blew the whistle, and the Badgers were back on the court. The ball was thrown in, and the Wildcats came out to play. A tall, mean-looking dude with serious eyebrows stole the ball from Grady's teammate Amir and drove it to their basket for an easy layup, not even looking for anyone to pass it to.

Closing in, Grady thought. He did everything he could to muster up some energy.

Brett threw the ball in, and the Wildcats moved in, full-court press. Number 11, the guy guarding Grady, was all over him, making it impossible for Grady to get clear to receive a pass.

"You guys are slipping," Number 11 said. "Might as well call it a day."

"This is parks and rec basketball, man," Grady said. "Save it for the big leagues."

The ball went wild, and one of the Badgers moved to stop it. He grabbed the ball but stepped out of bounds. The whistle blew. It was the Wildcats' ball.

"Perfect," Grady muttered. Now the Wildcats had the ball in their half of the court.

"Let's go, Badgers! Big D, big D!"

Even though Grady was tired, Number 11 had put the fight back into him.

The ball was passed back into play. The guy with the eyebrows grabbed it and shot an easy basket from inside the paint.

One more basket and the game will be tied, Grady thought.

As the Wildcats moved downcourt to get into a defensive zone, Eyebrows sneered at Grady.

"You call that Big D?" Eyebrows muttered.

"Game's not over yet," Grady snapped back.

"Might as well be," Eyebrows returned. "You guys are dead out here."

With those words, a secondary fire was lit inside of Grady Hopkins. As Brett passed the ball in, Grady looked up at the clock. There were 42 seconds left in the game. The Wildcats came in hard, doing everything they could to keep the ball in their half of the court.

Grady got a pass and drove it toward the center line. As he did, a hand reached in and slapped the ball free. Number 11 picked it up and drove it back toward the Wildcats' basket.

No! Grady thought. *No way!*

Grady spun and ran toward the basket. Number 11 dribbled around the right side as the key was loaded with players. Grady cut across and saw Number 11 getting ready to pop the ball up.

"Put it in, Grody!" one of the Wildcats shouted.

Were they talking to me? Grady thought briefly. Number 11's nickname sounded a lot like his own name. Using everything he had left, Grady jumped.

The ball was in the air, and Grady was airborne, too. He reached up and snatched the ball out of the sky, stealing it from midair.

The small crowd was on its feet, cheering. Grady landed and held the ball tight. He saw that Dominic, another one of his teammates, was open and bounced it his way. The Wildcats, still stunned from the steal, took a moment too long to react. Dominic was gone, headed toward Badger territory, where he made an easy layup. As the ball dropped through the net, the buzzer rang, sounding the end of the game.

"No!" Number 11 shouted. "C'mon, ref!"

A few of the Wildcats went over to the referee to complain, including Coach Dremble. They argued that Grady was goaltending and should be fouled. But it was no use. The score stood. The Badgers had won the championship!

2

ALWAYS SOMETHING

"You cheat!" one of the Wildcats shouted as the Badgers headed back to the bench. Some of the others hollered at them, too, but Grady couldn't hear them over the sounds of Coach Olson clapping and shouting praise their way.

"What a bunch of crybabies," Brett muttered, looking over his shoulder.

"No kidding," Grady agreed. "You'd think this was a professional tournament or something."

Coach Olson clapped each of the boys on the back and then ushered them back to the court to shake hands with the other team. As they lined up and said "good game, good game" over and over, Grady came up to Number 11.

"Good game, man," Grady said.

"Whatever," Number 11 snapped, withdrawing his hand. "You stink, Hopkins."

Eyebrows wouldn't slap his hand either.

"Lame move, loser," Eyebrows grunted. "That was goaltending."

"Whatever," Grady said. "The ball wasn't on its way down. He shot it, and I stole it. Consult a rule book, maybe?"

The Wildcats didn't say anything more as the teams returned to their benches. Grady could feel the heat from their stares as they left the gym and headed to get on their bus back to Brock County.

"There's losing and then there's sore losing," Brett said to Grady as they climbed into the bus.

"You're not kidding," Grady said, looking back at the school. "Now I wish we would've beat 'em by twenty points."

Way to ruin a perfectly good win, Grady thought. After a few minutes on the road and hearing his teammates recount their victory, he forgot all about Eyebrows and Number 11.

A little more than a week later, Grady was sitting behind a keyboard in the Wheatley Middle School computer lab. He and the rest of the Codeheads, the name he'd given to the after-school coding club he'd joined, were in the final stages of their projects.

"If this doesn't work, I'm going to lose it," Grady said. He'd just arranged the tables on his website the way he wanted them. The menu tabs all looked good and were readable against his web page's background. The links responded when he moused over them. Grady clicked the link that said VIDEOS, which was supposed to take visitors to a page where he'd put a bunch of the funniest video clips he'd found on the net.

Except it didn't.

He got a *PAGE NOT FOUND 404* error code, a pop-up window telling him that his page wasn't working right.

"Ugh!" Grady shouted. "Seriously?"

Ava Rhodes came over from her seat near the front of the computer lab.

"What happened, Hopkins?" Ava asked, folding her arms and looking at the error window. "Oh. Did you add the correct link attribute?"

"Yes? No?" Grady sighed and flipped to another window that showed all of the web links he wanted to display. "I don't know. Ugh. Maybe I should've taken piano lessons instead."

Grady sat back and watched as Ava took over for a moment. She closed the pop-up window, accessed his file server, and added the links to the videos.

"You just have to make sure to give these links a destination to point to," Ava said. "Otherwise it's going to error out, every time."

Grady nodded. It sounded like something he'd heard before, but for some reason, it hadn't stuck. He was surprised Ava wasn't giving him a harder time about it. She usually liked to throw jabs at him whenever she could.

"Okay, cool," Grady said. "Thanks, Ava."

"No problem," Ava said and smiled. "I'm just glad you're making a funny videos website and not some sort of national defense system. Otherwise, we'd all be in trouble."

Grady gave her a fake laugh.

"You should have a sitcom," Grady said. "Seriously. Those jokes are priceless."

Ava gave him a dirty look and went back to her seat.

Marco Martinez was busy at the workstation next to her. He was tinkering with his micro-bot, Mike, trying to get it to follow the command list he'd built. Grady sighed. The notion of building a robot or developing his own video game seemed like a long way off for him.

Before long, it was time to go. Grady saved his repaired and updated progress, packed his backpack, and walked home.

When Grady got home, his mom was waiting for him at the kitchen table.

"Hey, Mom," Grady said, setting his bag down and going to the fridge for a can of soda.

"Close the refrigerator and sit down, young man," his mom said. "We need to have a talk."

3

BAD REPORT

Grady knew the tone of his mom's voice well. This was the same tone she'd used when he'd turned his sister Becky's dollhouse into a house of horrors. It looked like some sort of twisted maniac had been turned loose in the tiny rooms, and Grady had ended up grounded for two weeks.

"Whatever it is," Grady began, pulling a chair out so he could sit, "I didn't do it. It's probably Becky's fault."

His mom didn't say a word but simply held up a sheet of paper. Grady instantly recognized it as his report card.

"Oh, that," Grady mumbled.

"Are you kidding me with these grades, Grady?" His mom turned the paper around and squinted at it to read them. Grady watched her, bracing himself for impact as she went through the list.

"Math, D," his mom read aloud. "Social studies, D."

"What?" Grady cried, genuinely shocked. "That's not possible!"

"Which one?"

"Both of them!" Grady replied, sitting up in his chair.

"Oh, we're just getting started," his mom snapped back. "History, D minus. English, D minus. Science, D. Physical education, F!"

"Whoa, whoa," Grady said, standing up from his chair. He felt like he'd been electrocuted.

"There's more," his mom said. "Your PE teacher wrote a comment: 'Grady smells terrible, too.'"

"What?" Grady came around the table to look at the report card himself. There was no way that comment was really there. He wondered if it was time for his mom to get an eye exam. "Are you serious?"

"I'm a little surprised that your teacher would say that," his mom admitted. "But it's here on the report card."

"This is ridiculous," Grady said, seeing the words for himself.

"I told you to bring your gym clothes home to be washed," his mom lectured. "Bring a couple sets so you always have something fresh to wear. Old sweaty gym clothes end up smelling like old taco meat."

"That's gross," Grady said, shaking the visual and scent description from his head. "But it's also crazy. I'm crushing it in PE, and my clothes aren't that funky yet, Mom!"

Grady's mom rubbed her eyes as if seeing Grady's horrible grades was too much for them to take.

"So what's the explanation for these other grades?" his mom asked. "It looks like if you don't get your act together, you're going to fail a few of these classes."

Grady picked up the report card and looked at it. The grades were exactly as his mom had read them. It didn't make sense. He was usually floating right around the C range in most of his classes and always scored an A in PE.

"There has to be a mistake," Grady said. "I don't think any of these grades are right."

His mom sighed and shook her head.

"It's there on the paper, plain as day," she said. "What are you going to do about it?"

Grady stared at the sheet and blinked, hoping the whole thing was a nightmare or some sort of trick someone was playing on him.

"I'm going to do something," Grady said. "Figure this out, somehow."

The next day, Grady walked into the school office with his report card in his hand. The secretary, Mrs. Yassin, looked up from her desk.

"Can I help you, Mr. Hopkins?"

"Yeah, hi," Grady said, holding up his report card. "I need to talk to someone about my report—"

"Oh, dear," Mrs. Yassin said, scrunching her lips up in a twist. "Not another one."

Grady looked at the sheet of paper in his hand and then back up at the secretary.

"What? What do you mean?"

Mrs. Yassin pointed. Sitting in all of the visitors' chairs and lined up outside the office of Mr. Brickman, the vice principal, were eight other sixth-grade students.

"What happened?" Grady asked, looking at the crowd. He recognized Maya Barba, easily the smartest student in Wheatley Middle School, sitting in a chair. She looked like she'd recently been crying.

"They're all claiming their report cards are incorrect," Mrs. Yassin whispered, as if it were a big secret. "So if you'll just find a space to wait, Mr. Brickman will be with you shortly."

"I've never gotten less than an A in my entire life!" Maya cried to anyone who cared to listen. "This is going to ruin my academic career forever. I'll end up living in a cardboard box for the rest of my life!"

Grady had to tune her out after a few moments. He was happy to get Cs, but he knew he could do better if he put the time and energy into it. Even so, hearing the school's smartest girl act like it was the end of the world was a bit much for him.

"I just don't understand this," Peter Yeboah said. "It's like we're being punished for our hard work by receiving poor grades."

As if that were the tipping point, Maya burst into tears again.

Wow, Grady thought. *What is going on?*

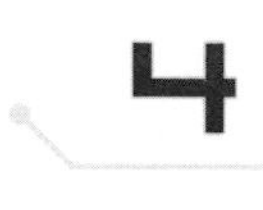

NOT THE ONLY ONE

"You too, eh, Grady?"

Grady turned and saw Brett, his friend and teammate from the Badgers basketball team, leaning against the office counter. He had the familiar folded piece of paper in his hand, too.

"Yeah," Grady said. "It's crazy, right? What the heck is happening?"

Brett shrugged and folded his report card up as if he didn't want anyone else to see it. Grady thought that was odd, considering that if he was one of the students in line to see Mr. Brickman, the grades on his report card were incorrect, too.

"I'm thinking it must be some sort of computer glitch," Brett said. "But you're in that computer club thing, aren't you? Is that something that could actually happen?"

"Ha, ha," Grady said. He wasn't sure if Brett was trying to make fun of him for his choice in after-school activity. "It could be something with the computer, but I don't know. It seems pretty strange that the computer would put something personal in the comments field."

Brett's eyebrows rose an inch. "What? What did yours say?"

"Oh, man," Grady grumbled, holding his report card out for Brett to read. "Check it out."

"'Grady smells terrible, too,'" Brett read aloud.

"Dude," Grady whispered, "not so loud!"

A few of the other students snickered. Maya let out a loud audible sigh. Knowing that she usually clocked straight As in all of her classes, Grady was curious as to what the "computer glitch" had given her.

"An F in phys ed?" Brett said, shaking his head. "Wow, this computer was really out to get you. I went from As and Bs to Cs. Nothing this bad."

Grady lowered his report card and exhaled. He would've been happy with his usual Cs. His mom would've been happy with that, too. As it stood, he was just as confused and wronged as the rest of the students in the office.

After talking with some of the others, Grady discovered that he had the lowest grades. Maya's had only dropped from As to Cs.

"I'll never get into college now," she moaned before bursting into tears again.

After most of the first period was over, Mr. Brickman finally came out to address Grady and the eight students who'd been the victims of the "computer glitch."

"Thank you, students, for waiting so patiently," Mr. Brickman said. He buttoned the front of his sports coat and then unbuttoned it as he talked. "We've pulled up the report cards for all of you and are going to be working with your teachers to determine which of the grades are accurate and which of them are incorrect."

REPORT CARD

"They're *all* incorrect," Maya cried. Tears streamed out of her eyes, making little rivers along her cheeks.

"I understand your concern, Ms. Barba," Mr. Brickman said, with little-to-no sympathy in his voice. "As I said, we'll make the corrections once we've conferred with your teachers. We'll get to the bottom of this problem so that it doesn't happen again."

"Can you find out why the computer decided to tell me I smell bad?" Grady asked. By then, everyone in the group knew what his report card said. "Because for the record, I smell delicious."

The students standing around laughed at his joke. All of them except Maya.

"We'll look into it, Mr. Hopkins," the vice principal promised. "I'm sure you smell just fine."

After informing the students that there would be no more questions, Mr. Brickman returned to his office.

"Well, this is just great!" Maya cried, storming away. "Why not just ruin my life some more?"

Brett looked at Grady and raised his eyebrows again.

"A bit dramatic, isn't she?"

"Yeah," Grady said. "She needs to calm down. It's not like the grades are going to stand. Still, I'd like to find out what the heck happened. This so-called glitch made it personal."

"Eh," Brett said as they followed the rest of the students out of the office. "I don't care. As long as they change them back."

Something occurred to Grady just then.

"Hey Brett," he said. "Isn't it weird that it just messed up the report cards for students in sixth grade? I mean, how come there weren't any seventh or eighth graders in there with errors? Why just us? And why were there only nine of us? There must be around 200 sixth graders, right?"

Brett shrugged. "How should I know? You're the computer whiz kid, aren't you?"

Not quite, Grady thought. *But I know some.*

5

GLITCHED!

At the end of social studies class, Grady hung back as the other students streamed into the hallway. Ms. Rollins looked up and gave him a smile.

"Can I help you with something, Grady?"

"Yes," Grady replied. "I wanted to ask you about my report card. I'm not sure if you heard about the grade mix-up."

Ms. Rollins looked puzzled. "I hadn't heard," she said. "Was there a dispute of some sort about the grade you received?"

Without waiting for an answer, she pulled a spiral notebook from her desk and opened it up, flipping to a specific page.

"So, my report card, along with the report cards for a few other students, had really low grades posted for the semester," Grady explained.

"Well," Ms. Rollins said, looking at something in her notebook, "like I've said during conferences, I think if you would apply yourself just a bit more, you'd be able to bring it up to a B fairly easily."

Grady took a deep breath and smiled.

"From a D?"

Ms. Rollins looked confused. "Well, I certainly didn't give you a D. I had you marked for a—"

"I'm pretty sure I was getting a C," Grady said, interrupting. "But that's the thing. A whole group of sixth graders ended up getting bad grades. Even Maya Barba. Mr. Brickman said he's going to look into it, so it'll probably be fine. Even so, I was curious. How do you put the grades in?"

"We have a program we use here at the school, or we can access it remotely from

home by getting into the school's network," Ms. Rollins explained.

"So do you have a special log-in or something?"

"Yes," Ms. Rollins explained. "Each teacher has a different password, and when we log in, we can see all of the classes we're teaching and the individual students in each one. It's a pretty fancy system."

Grady nodded.

"Why do you ask?" Ms. Rollins put her notebook down and seemed to study Grady carefully.

"Just trying to do some investigating on my own," he said. "My mom was pretty upset. I had all Ds and an F in PE."

"Oh, my," Ms. Rollins said, shaking her head. "Well, I'll be able to confirm with

Mr. Brickman that you're sitting on a solid C in my class. But you could get to a B—"

Grady nodded. "I know," he said. "And I'll do my best."

The bell rang. Grady thanked Ms. Rollins and headed for his locker.

Dead end, he thought.

Though Mr. Brickman was "on the case," Grady couldn't help but check with each of his teachers to make sure the grade that showed up wasn't the one he was supposed to be getting. In every instance, the grade on his report card was lower than what they'd put into the system.

By the end of the day, everyone in the school knew about the computer glitch. As Grady walked into the computer room for coding club, all of the members of the Codeheads were already seated.

All of them were plugging their noses.

"Wow!" said Travis Jacobson from the back. "Is that you who stinks, Grady?"

"Very funny," Grady replied. He couldn't help but smile.

Dang, he thought. *I go to school with some legendary bigmouths!*

"Hey, Hopkins," Ava said, her nose still plugged. "We're going to pitch in and get you some deodorant. Will you promise to use it?"

"Yeah, yeah. Hilarious," Grady said, not wanting to waste any time. "Any computer nerds in the house have any ideas about how this computer glitch happened?"

"Let's stop with the computer *nerd* business, okay?" Mrs. Donovan said. "We're all computer *enthusiasts*."

Mrs. Donovan smiled. Grady knew she was kidding. Everyone in the coding club embraced the nickname. *Nerd* wasn't a bad word in their circles, but a badge of honor.

"We were talking about this before you came in, Grady," Marco added, angling his wheelchair so he could see Grady. "And we came up with a couple of different theories."

Miles Patrick turned around in his seat. "It's no glitch, dude. You need to study more."

"Whatever," Grady said, waving him off. Some of the others in the group laughed at his dig.

Marco smiled and seemed to wait for everyone to calm down. He looked at something on his laptop and pressed a key.

"My theory on the whole matter is quite simple," Marco said.

"Simple?" Grady asked. "How?"

"There's no computer glitch that would cause a handful of students to get lower grades," Marco said plainly.

"Except it happened," Grady said. "So that theory is blown out of the water."

"Not exactly," Marco replied. "There must be a correlation to the students who were victims."

"Yeah," Grady said. "All of them were in sixth grade."

"True," Ava added. "But wasn't there a nasty comment about your body odor on there, too?"

"Okay," Grady snapped. "For the record, I don't have body odor. But yes, there was a comment."

"A glitch wouldn't single you out and make such a statement," Marco concluded. "And so, the obvious answer is simple. The grading system was hacked."

ALGORITHMS

***Hacked?* Grady thought.** *How is that even possible? And who would want to hack the school's grading system?*

Mrs. Donovan smiled at Marco after he'd come up with the theory as if he were her star pupil. Grady supposed that if the coding club were an actual class and not just an after-school activity, he would be. Ava Rhodes was right up there, too.

"It's possible that someone was able to find a way into the website where the grades are posted," Mrs. Donovan said. "But it seems an odd choice to hack something like this. Usually hackers are looking to steal money or identities or cause havoc of some sort."

"Have you seen my hacked report card?" Grady asked, fishing it out of his backpack. "It caused plenty of havoc at my house. My mom is ready to send me to one of those military schools."

"Oh, Mr. Hopkins," Mrs. Donovan laughed. "I'm sure she wouldn't do something like that. She'd miss you too much."

Grady shrugged. "Yeah, maybe. Some days not so much."

"Well, it shouldn't be too hard to figure out who logged into the system and made the changes," Marco chimed in. "We could do a search of the IP addresses that modified the records at a certain time."

Grady's head was spinning a bit.

"What? IP addresses? What's that?" he asked.

"An IP address is a number that's assigned to a device using the Internet," Ava explained. "IP stands for Internet Protocol."

"Exactly," Marco said. "So think of an IP address like a house address of sorts. The number identifies where it's coming from and where it's going to, allowing two different houses to send mail to each other."

"The IP addresses are like fingerprints, telling the network who and what accessed the system and when," Ava added.

"Perfect," Grady said. "So we dust the Internet for fingerprints? Just like those crime scene investigator people on TV?"

"Kind of," Ava said. "We could develop some sort of quick program to help us out."

Grady nodded. "Okay," he said, "that's pretty sweet. So all we have to do is pull up all of the IP addresses, right? What do these addresses look like? Will it have the user's name in there?"

Marco shook his head.

"Not really," he explained. "It's more like a series of four numbers from 0 to 255. The problem is that there are going to be

IP addresses for anyone who's gone in. From there, we have to figure out which number belongs to who. Each IP address should be registered to the system, so they should all be from the school—"

"Oh, and some of those address thingies might be from a teacher's house, too," Grady said. "Ms. Rollins said some teachers post their grades from home if they don't have time to do it while they're here."

"This could be kind of tricky," Ava said. "A teacher could have an IP address for their classroom computer and their home computer. They might even log in from a tablet."

"So, that's like a ton of IP addresses," Tara Calhoun mumbled, looking up from her cell phone. "If they're going to fix the grades back to what you should've gotten, why bother messing with all this?"

"Because justice needs to be served!" Grady said, faking his passion a bit for comedic effect. "I want to know who decided to mess with me!"

"C'mon, Grady," Travis said. "That's a bit much, don't you think?"

Mrs. Donovan smiled. "Well, the good news is, Mr. Brickman asked me to assist. I told him that we'd discuss this in our coding club and see what we come up with."

Marco made a few clicking noises with his tongue. Grady noticed he did that when the gears were turning in his brain.

"Did he give us access to the site?" Grady asked.

"Read-only access," Mrs. Donovan said. "We won't be able to access or change any of the student grades, but we'll be able to see how many users have logged on, when they did, and whose records they've accessed."

"So we'll get those address thingies?" Grady asked.

"Oh, yes," Marco said. "It'll be interesting to see what we come up with."

Once Mrs. Donovan gave them a temporary log-in to the site, Grady pulled his chair over to Marco's workstation, and Ava drew in close, too. The rest of the Codeheads, although interested, were busy with their own projects.

"Okay," Marco said. "First, the scary part. Let's do a search to see how many IP addresses have gone into the site in the last few weeks."

Marco accessed the site's administrator screens and ran off a quick report. Within seconds, the screen was flooded with numbers. There didn't seem to be any rhyme or reason to them.

"That's a lot of IP addresses," Ava said.

"Wait," Grady said. He unfolded his report card and scanned the paper. "Wouldn't it make more sense to just do a search around the date the report cards were printed?"

"That could significantly change the range of addresses accessing the system," Marco said, and then asked, "Is there one on there?"

At the bottom of the page, Grady found a small date. "Yeah. Here!"

Marco changed the parameters, and they were given a smaller number of addresses. Even so, it was more than they were willing to sift through.

"Another dead end," Grady groaned. *Are we ever going to figure this out?*

7

SURPRISE!

Though Grady was frustrated, Marco wasn't ready to give up.

"There has to be a way to narrow it down even more," Marco said. "Right now we're getting every computer or device that accessed the site on the date the grades were posted."

"How about I write down the names of the people who complained about their report cards?" Grady suggested. "That way we're only looking at nine student records, including mine."

Ava nodded and smiled at Grady before giving him a playful punch in the shoulder.

"Look at you go, Hopkins," she said. "You really want to figure this out, don't you?"

"Well, yeah," Grady said, writing down the names of students he'd seen waiting for Mr. Brickman. He made sure to include Maya Barba and Brett Robbins, too. "If someone was looking to wreck your grades and insult your personal hygiene, you'd want to know who it was, wouldn't you?"

"Oh, yeah," Ava said.

Marco entered the names of each student record and copied the IP addresses from the results. He opened a spreadsheet and dumped the numbers into the columns. There were considerably fewer addresses to sift through.

Ava went to her computer and started typing.

"Hey," Grady said, "I thought you were helping, too."

"I am," Ava said. "I'm putting together an algorithm that will look for repeated hits in each of the student records. I'll filter the IP addresses that modified every one of the records."

"Okay," Grady said. What she was saying sort of made sense. "So you'll be able to see which teachers belong to each student?"

Ava nodded. "Yep," she replied. "And if this works right, we'll be able to remove the teachers from the mix. With a little luck, we should be left with an IP address that shows up in all of the hacked student records."

A lightbulb just about exploded inside Grady's head.

"And that IP address should be our culprit, right?"

Marco and Ava both nodded like a couple of bobbleheads.

Grady sat back and watched, his mind working overtime. He started to think about the low-down snake in the grass who tried to mess with him and some of the other sixth graders at Wheatley Middle School.

Are they sitting at home right now, thinking they got away with it?

Grady wondered what the hacker's face would look like when the Codeheads caught them and waved the proof of their investigation under their nose. He hoped that if and when they solved the hack attack on their school's grading system, he'd be able to be there for the bust. Grady didn't know what sort of laws there were about hacking, but he figured they were pretty serious.

An F in PE class? Who is the hacker kidding with that? Making him "fail" PE was a serious enough offense!

Marco motioned Grady over, and the two of them looked at what they had come up with. Together they identified the classes and who the teachers were for each class. It was complicated, but it made sense. Because they had a number of different teachers for each class, it looked like there were a ton of different IP addresses accessing each student account.

Ava organized the data into three tables. One was a column with all of the student IDs. The second was the IP address that entered the grades for each student. The last column was the teacher IDs along with their IP addresses. All of the data was making Grady's head spin.

"We'll put these in a CSV format," Marco explained.

"Marco, buddy, you're driving me crazy with all of these TLAs," Grady grumbled.

"TLA?" Marco replied, looking puzzled for the first time Grady could remember. "I'm not sure I know what—"

"Three Letter Acronym," Grady said with a quick grin. "So help me out here. What's a CSV?"

Marco laughed and nodded. "Okay, okay. Sorry. CSV stands for Comma Separated Value. Here, it'll look something like this."

Grady watched as Marco typed an example on his laptop screen and then pointed at it.

"It'll be student name, ID number, and then the IP address," Marco explained.

Grady H, 1234, 143.23.3677.445

"This makes it easier for the computer to understand," Ava explained.

"Right. We'll put their names in the table and see which IP address belongs to which teacher. We can run down the list and figure out which IP addresses belong to each student ID."

"It should help us reveal our hacker a lot quicker," Ava said.

Grady watched as they moved their data around. One by one, the names associated with each IP address began to fill the spreadsheet. He watched as little by little, the IP addresses were filtered from the list.

"Okay," Grady said, following along. "So is that all of them?"

Marco took a deep breath and looked at both Ava and Grady.

"Nope," he said. "There's one more here."

Grady felt a surge of excitement course through his entire body.

It's go time, he thought. *You're going down, hacker scum!*

"This last IP address was in all of the grading sections of the nine students you listed, including you. They accessed each grade posted for each of them," Marco said quietly. "Whoever this person is, they definitely changed the grades."

"And wrote that you stink, Hopkins," Ava reminded him, laughing.

Marco hovered over the button that would ping the network and send him back the name of the user who owned the device the IP address belonged to.

"Holy cow, the anticipation is killing me," Grady said. "Click it already, Marco."

Marco clicked the link. The status bar moved along swiftly, and the new screen loaded. In seconds they would know who the hacker was.

Grady blinked. When his eyes opened again, the hacker was revealed.

"Principal Grodichuk?" he said out loud.

CONFESSION

"You've got to be kidding me," Grady said. "The hacker is Principal Grodichuk? Is that even possible?"

"What did you guys find out?" Mrs. Donovan said, walking over to Marco's workstation. The three of them continued to stare at the screen, dumbfounded by their discovery. The rest of the coding club was crowded around, too.

"According to our data, Principal Grodichuk is the one who went in and modified the grades," Marco said. He flipped to his other screens, checking his work. All the while, he shook his head in disbelief.

"Well, that's . . . ," Mrs. Donovan said. "There has to be some mistake."

"No way," Tara said. "Why would the principal do something like that? I mean, she's the principal!"

Marco flipped through some other tabs in the grading software and found a screen for approving the grades. Grady watched as he did a search, revealing two other IP addresses.

"It looks like she routinely goes into the system to approve the grades once the teacher posts them," Marco said. "But it doesn't make sense that she'd go into the actual grade entry screen."

"Yeah," Grady said. "And why just these eight students and me? Why not everyone? It's too big of a coincidence."

Grady sat back in his chair, feeling defeated. There was something wrong. He knew there was no way the principal would change grades just for the heck of it. She wasn't an evil lady.

"Could someone have hacked Principal Grodichuk's account?" Ava asked, looking up at their adviser. "Or maybe logged in as her on her computer?"

Mrs. Donovan shrugged. "I guess it's possible," she replied. "But it comes back down to why? Why would someone go through the trouble just to play a cruel prank and say mean things about Grady's hygiene?"

Unless, Grady thought. *Maybe it wasn't all that much trouble after all.*

"Can you think of anyone who might be out to get you, Grady?" Marco asked. "Anyone you might have made mad?"

Grady thought. The only person he could think of who was mad at him recently was his mom. She was mad that just about every one of his grades had been a big D.

Big D . . .

Grady's eyes widened, and his mind began to spin. He grabbed Marco's laptop and pulled up a search window. He typed the words *basketball* and *Grodichuk* into the search field.

"What are you doing?" Marco asked. "I'm not sure I foll—"

"Give me a second."

Grady hit SEARCH and scrolled through the results. He found the parks and recreation site where both search items were flagged. Clicking on the link, Grady sifted through the site.

"No way," Grady said.

Ava leaned in to see what he was looking for. "Okay, seriously, how is this supposed to help, Hopkins?"

You stink, Hopkins!

Grady smiled and clicked on a link showing the different basketball teams that

had played in the tournament his parks and recreation team had won a little more than a week ago.

"This," Grady said, pointing at the team rosters. He scanned the names for the Wilbur County Wildcats and saw a name they all recognized.

Corey Grodichuk. Number 11.

"I don't get it," Ava said.

"That guy. That's our hacker," Grady said. "I'll bet my life on it."

"I don't understand," Mrs. Donovan said, still trying to put it together. "Why would Mrs. Grodichuk's son be our hacker? It seems like a wild shot."

Grady took a deep breath and told the whole story. The entire Codeheads crew listened in. When he got to the end, Grady connected the dots.

"So, Principal Grodichuk's son was super angry that I stole the ball while their team was trying to tie it up," Grady said. "He even said 'You stink, Hopkins!' I didn't think anything of it, but that makes sense, why he put that in the comments of my report card."

Marco nodded, clicking his tongue a bit as he processed the new theory.

"You didn't see his last name on the back of his jersey?" Ava asked.

"No," Grady said. "Their team didn't have names on theirs, just numbers. Ours did. That's how he knew who I was. At one point, someone on his team called him 'Grody.' I remember it because at first I thought he was talking to me. But 'Grody' must be Corey Grodichuk's nickname."

"It seems possible," Marco said. "Maybe while Principal Grodichuk was approving the grades, he somehow got into the system."

"Sure," Ava said. "She's the boss. She probably has the ability to get into every student's record. You think he found her password or something?"

Grady thought about that. She didn't seem like the kind of person who would leave something that important lying around.

"Maybe she stepped away from her computer or something," Grady thought. "You know. Didn't log off or whatever."

"But why go after other students?" Ava asked. "Why not just you?"

"He changed Brett's grades, too," Grady replied. "Brett was on my basketball team. In fact, we're the only ones from Wheatley on the team. As for the others, maybe he didn't want it to seem so obvious."

The room was silent.

"Wow," Ava said. "We're going to accuse Mrs. Grodichuk's son of hacking into the school's system."

"Technically, it's not a full-on hack," Marco said. "It's just sneaking onto his mom's computer."

"Sounds cooler when we call him a hacker," Ava said. "Don't you think?"

"Well," Mrs. Donovan said, exhaling. "This will be a tough conversation. I'll see if she's still in the office."

As Mrs. Donovan left the room, Grady had mixed feelings.

What if we're wrong?

That night, there was a knock on the front door of the Hopkins house. A moment later, Grady's mom called him downstairs.

Uh-oh, Grady thought. *This can't be good.*

Standing at the door were two people: Principal Grodichuk and her son, Number 11. Corey Grodichuk.

"I'm sorry to bother you at home, Mr. Hopkins," his principal said. "But my son would like to apologize to you."

Grady felt his face get hot and red. He never expected something like this to happen so quickly.

"I'm sorry," Corey mumbled, barely able to look Grady in the eye.

"Yeah, okay," Grady replied. He wasn't sure what else to say.

"I got mad about the game and everything," Corey said, looking down at his feet. "I thought it would be funny to mess with you. It wasn't cool, and I apologize."

Grady nodded.

"Corey got onto my computer when I was approving grades last Sunday," Principal Grodichuk explained. "I took an important phone call, and he got onto the grading screen. I am so sorry this happened, Grady. I will understand if you want to press charges—"

"Oh, no," Grady said. "No, no. We don't need to do that."

Corey nodded and actually smiled a bit.

"Apology accepted," Grady said. "But there is one thing I would like. Corey and I have unfinished business."

Corey looked up, and his eyebrows rose. "What? What do you mean?"

Grady held his right hand up. "Good game, man."

Corey laughed and high-fived Grady.

"Yeah," he said. "Good game, Hopkins."

THE END

THINK ABOUT IT

1. When Grady is playing basketball, he's worn out and ready to give up. What happens that makes him want to try and win? Use evidence in the story to support your answer.

2. The comment on Grady's report card is something a teacher would never write. Does anyone actually believe his PE teacher wrote this? Use examples from the book as proof.

3. When Grady confronts the hacker at the end of the book, we see that Grady is a good sport. What does he do?

WRITE ABOUT IT

1. In this book, Grady is the target of someone looking for revenge. Have you ever had someone really mad at you for something you did? What was it? Be sure to include these details in your story.

2. The coding club is asked to help figure out who hacked the grading system. Write a story about a time you were asked to help out with something important. What was your mission? Include details in your story.

3. Grady forgives the hacker for messing with his grades. Write about a time when you forgave someone. What did he or she do? Why did you decide to forgive him or her?

ABOUT THE AUTHOR

Thomas Kingsley Troupe started writing stories when he was in second grade. Since then, he's authored more than sixty fiction and nonfiction books for kids. Born and raised in "Nordeast" Minneapolis, he now lives in Woodbury, Minnesota. In his spare time, he enjoys spending time with his family, conducting paranormal investigations, and watching movies with the Friends of Cinema. One of his favorite words is *delicious*.

ABOUT THE ILLUSTRATOR

Scott Burroughs graduated from the San Francisco, California, Academy of Art University in 1994 with a BFA in illustration. Upon graduating, he was hired by Sega of America as a conceptual artist and animator. In 1995, he completed the Walt Disney Feature Animation Internship program and was hired as an animator. While at Disney, he was an animator, a mentor for new artists, and a member of the Portfolio Review Board. He worked at the Disney Florida Studio until it closed its doors in 2005. Since 2005, Scott has been illustrating everything from children's books to advertisements and editorials, just to name a few. Scott is also a published author of several children's books. He resides in northern California with his high school sweetheart/wife and two sons.

MORE FUN WITH THE CODING CLUB

GAMER BANDIT

When a mysterious lunch thief leaves behind a card with a website address, Ava Rhodes can't help but check it out. After the site leads her to a really boring online video game, she's even more determined. Can GPS tracking help Ava and her friends find the thief? Or will more lunches go missing?

NABBED TABLET

When Ava Rhodes's brand-new tablet computer goes missing, she's desperate to solve the mystery. Can her fellow coding club members Marco and Grady and some quick coding help her? Or is everyone a suspect?

SCHOOL SPIRIT

When weird noises in the school's media center have students spooked, Marco Martinez is on the case. Marco writes up a code to alert him to any ghost-like activity. But does he have more than ghosts to be afraid of?
